Greylorn

Greylorn

by Keith Laumer

Start Publishing PD LLC
Copyright © 2024 by Start Publishing PD LLC

All rights reserved, including the right to reproduce this book or portions
thereof in any form whatsoever.

Start Publishing PD is a registered trademark of Start Publishing PD LLC
Manufactured in the United States of America

Cover art: Shutterstock/Taisiya Kozorez

Cover design: Jennifer Do

10 9 8 7 6 5 4 3 2 1

ISBN 979-8-8809-0519-5

Table of Contents

Prologue

The murmur of conversation around the conference table died as the World Secretary entered the room and took his place at the head of the table.

"Ladies and Gentlemen," he said. "I'll not detain you with formalities today. The representative of the Navy Department is waiting outside to present the case for his proposal. You all know something of the scheme; it has been heard and passed as feasible by the Advisory Group. It will now be our responsibility to make the decision. I ask that each of you in forming a conclusion remember that our present situation can only be described as desperate, and that desperate measures may be in order."

The Secretary turned and nodded to a braided admiral seated near the door who left the room and returned a moment later with a young gray-haired Naval Officer.

"Members of the Council," said the admiral, "this is Lieutenant Commander Greylorn." All eyes followed the officer as he walked the length of the room to take the empty seat at the end of the table.

"Please proceed, Commander," said the Secretary.

"Thank you, Mr. Secretary." The Commander's voice was unhurried and low, yet it carried clearly and held authority. He began without preliminary.

"When the World Government dispatched the Scouting Forces forty-three years ago, an effort was made to contact each of the twenty-five worlds to which this government had sent Colonization parties during the Colonial Era of the middle Twentieth Centuries. With the return of the last of the scouts early this year, we were forced to realize that no assistance would be forthcoming from that source."

The Commander turned his eyes to the world map covering the wall. With the exception of North America and a narrow strip of coastal waters, the entire map was tinted an unhealthy pink.

"The latest figures compiled by the Department of the Navy indicate that we are losing area at the rate of one square mile every twenty-one hours. The organism's faculty for developing resistance to our chemical and biological measures appears to be evolving rapidly. Analyses of atmospheric samples indicate the level of noxious content rising at a steady rate. In other words, in spite of our best efforts, we are not holding our own against the Red Tide."

A mutter ran around the table, as Members shifted uncomfortably in their seats.

"A great deal of thought has been applied to the problem of increasing our offensive ability. This in the end is still a question of manpower and raw resources. We do not have enough. Our small improvements in effectiveness have been progressively offset by increasing casualties and loss of territory. In the end, alone, we must lose."

The Commander paused, as the murmur rose and died again. "There is however, one possibility still unexplored," he said. "And recent work done at the Polar Research Station places the possibility well within the scope of feasibility. At the time the attempt was made to establish contact with the colonies, one was omitted. It alone now remains to be sought out. I refer to the Omega Colony."

A portly Member leaned forward and burst out, "The location of the colony is unknown!"

The Secretary intervened. "Please permit the Commander to complete his remarks. There will be ample opportunity for discussion when he has finished."

"This contact was not attempted for two reasons," the Commander continued. "First, the precise location was not known; second, the distance was at least twice that of the earlier colonies. At the time, there was a feeling of optimism which seemed to make the attempt superfluous. Now the situation has changed. The possibility of contacting Omega Colony now assumes paramount importance.

"The development of which I spoke is a new application of drive principle which has given to us a greatly improved effective velocity for space propulsion. Forty years ago, the minimum elapsed time of return travel to the presumed sector within which the Omega World should lie was about a century. Today we have the techniques to construct a small scouting vessel capable of making the transit in just over five years. We cannot hold out here for a century, perhaps; but we can manage a decade.

"As for location, we know the initial target point toward which Omega was launched. The plan was of course that a precise target should be selected by the crew after approaching the star group closely enough to permit telescopic planetary resolution and study. There is no reason why the crew of a scout could not make the same study and examination of possible targets, and with luck find the colony.

"Omega was the last colonial venture undertaken by our people, two centuries after the others. It was the best equipped and largest expedition of them all. It was not limited to one destination, little known, but had a presumably large selection of potentials from which to choose; and her planetary study facilities were extremely advanced. I have full confidence that Omega made a successful planetfall and has by now established a vigorous new society.

"Honorable Members of the Council, I submit that all the resources of this Government should be at once placed at the disposal of a task force with the assigned duty of constructing a fifty-thousand-ton scouting vessel, and conducting an exhaustive survey of a volume of space of one thousand A.U.'s centered on the so-called Omega Cluster."

The World Secretary interrupted the babble which arose with the completion of the officer's presentation.

"Ladies and gentlemen, time is of the essence of our problem. Let's proceed at once to orderly interrogation. Mr. Klayle, lead off, please."

The portly Councillor glared at the Commander. "The undertaking you propose, sir, will require a massive diversion of our capacities from defense. That means losing ground at an increasing rate to the obscenity crawling over our planet. That same potential applied to direct offensive measures may yet turn the balance in our favor. Against this, the possibility of a scouting party stumbling over the remains of a colony the location of which is almost completely problematical, and which by analogy with all of the earlier colonial attempts has at best managed to survive as a marginal foothold, is so fantastically remote as to be inconsiderable."

The Commander listened coolly, seriously. "Mr. Councillor," he replied, "as to our defensive measures, we have passed the point of diminishing returns. We have more knowledge now than we are capable of employing against the plague. Had we not neglected the physical sciences as we have for the last two centuries, we might have developed adequate measures before we had been so far reduced in numbers and area as to be unable to produce and employ the new weapons our laboratories have belatedly developed. Now we must be realistic; there is no hope in that direction.

"As to the location of the Omega World, our plan is based on the fact that the selection was not made at random. Our scout will proceed along the Omega course line as known to us from the observations which were carried on for almost three years after its departure. We propose to continue on that line, carrying out systematic observation of each potential sun in turn. As we detect planets, we will alter course only as necessary to satisfy ourselves as to the possibility of suitability of the planet. We can safely assume that Omega will not have bypassed any likely target. If we should have more than one prospect under consideration at any time, we shall examine them in turn. If the Omega World has developed successfully, ample evidence should be discernible at a distance."

Klayle muttered "Madness," and subsided. The angular member on his left spoke gently, "Mr. Greylorn, why, if this colonial venture has met with the success you assume, has its government not reestablished contact with the mother world during the last two centuries?"

"On that score, Mr. Councillor, we can only conjecture," the Commander said. "The outward voyage may have required as much as fifty or sixty years. After that, there must have followed a lengthy period of development and expansion in building the new world. It is not to be expected that the pioneers would be ready to expend resources in expeditionary ventures for some time."

"I do not completely understand your apparent confidence in the ability of the hypothetical Omega culture to supply massive aid to us, even if its people should be so inclined," said a straight-backed woman member. "The time seems very short for the mastery of an alien world."

"The population development plan, Madam, provided for an increase from the original 10,000 colonists to approximately 40,000 within twenty years, after which the rate of increase would of course rapidly grow. Assuming sixty years for planetfall, the population should now number over one hundred sixty millions. Given population, all else follows."

Two hours later, the World Secretary summed up. "Ladies and gentlemen, we have the facts before us. There still exist differences in interpretation, which however will not be resolved by continued repetition. I now call for a vote on the resolution proposed by the Military Member and presented by Commander Greylorn."

There was silence in the Council Chamber as the votes were recorded and tabulated. Then the World Secretary sighed softly.

"Commander," he said, "the Council has approved the resolution. I'm sure that there will be general agreement that you will be placed at the head of the project, since you were director of the team which developed the new drive and are also the author of the plan. I wish you the best of luck." He rose and extended his hand.

The first keel plate of the Armed Courier Vessel Galahad was laid thirty-two hours later.

Chapter 1

I expected trouble when I left the bridge. The tension that had been building for many weeks was ready for release in violence. The ship was silent as I moved along the passageway. Oddly silent, I thought; something was brewing.

I stopped before the door of my cabin, listening; then I put my ear to the wall. I caught the faintest of sounds from within; a muffled click, voices. Someone inside, someone attempting to be very quiet. I was not overly surprised. Sooner or later the trouble had had to come into the open. I looked up the passage, dim in the green glow of the nightlights. There was no one in sight.

I listened. There were three voices, too faint to identify. The clever thing for me to do now would be to walk back up to the bridge, and order the Provost Marshall to clear my cabin, but I had an intuitive feeling that that was not the way to handle the situation. It would make things much simpler all around if I could push through this with as little commotion as possible.

There was no point in waiting. I took out my key and placed it soundlessly in the slot. As the door slid back I stepped briskly into the room. Kramer, the Medical Officer, and Joyce, Assistant Communications Officer, stood awkwardly, surprised. Fine, the Supply Officer, was sprawled on my bunk. He sat up quickly.

They were a choice selection. Two of them were wearing sidearms. I wondered if they were ready to use them, or if they knew just how far they were prepared to go. My task would be to keep them from finding out.

I avoided looking surprised. "Good evening, gentlemen," I said cheerfully. I stepped to the liquor cabinet, opened it, poured Scotch into a glass. "Join me in a drink?" I said.

None of them answered. I sat down. I had to move just a little faster than they did, and by holding the initiative, keep them off balance. They had counted on hearing my approach, having a few moments to get set, and using my surprise against me. I had reversed their play and taken the advantage. How long I could keep it depended on how well I played my few cards. I plunged ahead, as I saw Kramer take a breath and wrinkle his brow, about to make his pitch.

"The men need a change, a break in the monotony," I said. "I've been considering a number of possibilities." I fixed my eyes on Fine as I talked. He sat stiffly on the edge of my bunk. Already he was regretting his boldness in presuming to rumple the Captain's bed.

"It might be a good bit of drill to set up a few live missile runs on random targets," I said. "There's also the possibility of setting up a small arms range and qualifying all hands." I switched my eyes to Kramer. Fine was sorry he'd come, and Joyce wouldn't take the initiative; Kramer was my problem. "I see you have your Mark 9, Major," I said, holding out my hand. "May I see it?" I smiled pleasantly.

I hoped I had hit him quickly and smoothly enough, before he had had time to adjust to the situation. Even for a hard operator like Kramer, it took mental preparation to openly defy his Commander, particularly in casual conversation. But possession of the weapon was more than casual....

I looked at him, smiling, my hand held out. He wasn't ready; he pulled the pistol from its case, handed it to me.

I flipped the chamber open, glanced at the charge indicator, checked the action. "Nice weapon," I said. I laid it on the open bar at my right.

Joyce opened his mouth to speak. I cut in in the same firm snappy tone I use on the bridge. "Let me see yours, Lieutenant."

He flushed, looked at Kramer, then passed the pistol over without a word. I took it, turned it over thoughtfully, and then rose, holding it negligently by the grip.

"Now, if you gentlemen don't mind, I have a few things to attend to." I was not smiling. I looked at Kramer with expressionless eyes. "I think we'd better keep our little chat confidential for the present. I think I can promise you action in the near future, though."

They filed out, looking as foolish as three preachers caught in a raid on a brothel. I stood without moving until the door closed. Then I let my breath out. I sat down and finished off the Scotch in one drag.

"You were lucky, boy," I said aloud. "Three gutless wonders."

I looked at the Mark 9's on the table. A blast from one of those would have burned all four of us in that enclosed room. I dumped them into a drawer and loaded my Browning 2mm. The trouble wasn't over yet, I knew. After this farce, Kramer would have to make another move to regain his prestige. I unlocked the door, and left it slightly ajar. Then I threw the main switch and stretched out on my bunk. I put the Browning needler on the little shelf near my right hand.

Perhaps I had made a mistake, I reflected, in eliminating formal discipline as far as possible in the shipboard routine. It had seemed the best course for a long cruise under the present conditions. But now I had a morale situation that could explode in mutiny at the first blunder on my part.

I knew that Kramer was the focal point of the trouble. He was my senior staff officer, and carried a great deal of weight in the Officer's Mess. As a medic, he knew most of the crew better than I. I thought I knew Kramer's driving motive, too. He had always been a great success with the women. When he had volunteered for the mission he had doubtless pictured himself as quite a romantic hero, off on a noble but hopeless quest. Now, after four years in deep space, he was beginning to realize that he was getting no younger, and that at best he would have spent a decade of his prime in monastic seclusion. He wanted to go back now, and salvage what he could.

It was incredible to me that this movement could have gathered followers, but I had to face the fact; my crew almost to a man had given up the search before it was well begun. I had heard the first rumors only a few weeks before, but the idea had spread through the crew like wildfire. Now, I couldn't afford drastic action, or risk forcing a blowup by arresting ringleaders. I had to baby the situation along with an easy hand and hope for good news from the Survey Section. A likely find now would save us.

There was still every reason to hope for success in our search. To date all had gone according to plan. We had followed the route of Omega as far as it had been charted, and then gone on, studying the stars ahead for evidence of planets. We had made our first finds early in the fourth year of the voyage. It had been a long tedious time since then of study and observation, eliminating one world after another as too massive, too cold, too close to a blazing primary, too small to hold an atmosphere. In all we had discovered twelve planets, of four suns. Only one had looked good enough for close observation. We had moved in to televideo range before realizing it was an all-sea world.

Now we had five new main-sequence suns ahead within six months' range. I hoped for a confirmation on a planet at any time. To turn back now to a world that had pinned its last hopes on our success was unthinkable, yet this was Kramer's plan, and that of his followers. They would not prevail while I lived. Still it was not my plan to be a party to our failure through martyrdom. I intended to stay alive and carry through to success. I dozed lightly and waited.

I awoke when they tried the door. It had swung open a few inches at the touch of the one who had tried it, not expecting it to be unlatched. It stood ajar now, the pale light from the hall shining on the floor. No one entered. Kramer was still fumbling, unsure of himself. At every surprise with which I presented him, he was paralyzed, expecting a trap. Several minutes passed in tense silence; then the door swung wider.

"I'll be forced to kill the first man who enters this room," I said in a steady voice. I hadn't picked up the gun.

I heard urgent whispers in the hall. Then a hand reached in behind the shelter of the door and flipped the light switch. Nothing happened, since I had opened the main switch. It was only a small discomfiture, but it had the effect of interfering with their plan of action, such as it was. These men were being pushed along by Kramer, without a clearly thought out plan. They hardly knew how to go about defying lawful authority.

I called out, "I suggest you call this nonsense off now, and go back to your quarters, men. I don't know who is involved in this, yet. You can get away clean if you leave quietly, now, before you've made a serious mistake."

I hoped it would work. This little adventure, abortive though it was, might serve to let off steam. The men would have something to talk about for a few precious days. I picked up the needler and waited. If the bluff failed, I would have to kill someone.

Distantly I heard a metallic clatter. Moments later a tremor rattled the objects on the shelf, followed a few seconds later by a heavy shuddering. Papers slid from my desk, fluttered across the floor. The whiskey bottle toppled, rolled to the far wall. I felt dizzy, as my bunk seemed to tilt under me. I reached for the intercom key and flipped it.

"Taylor," I said, "this is the Captain. What's the report?"

There was a momentary delay before the answer came. "Captain, we've taken a meteor strike aft, apparently a metallic body. It must have hit us a tremendous wallop because it's set up a rotation. I've called out Damage Control."

"Good work, Taylor," I said. I keyed for Stores; the object must have hit about there. "This is the Captain," I said. "Any damage there?"

I got a hum of background noise, then a too-close transmission. "Uh, Cap'n, we got a hole in the aft bulkhead here. I slapped a seat pad over it. Man, that coulda killed somebody."

I flipped off the intercom and started aft at a run. My visitors had evaporated. In the passage men stood, milled, called questions. I keyed my mike as I ran. "Taylor, order all hands to emergency stations."

It was difficult running, since the floors had assumed an apparent tilt. Loose gear was rolling and sliding along underfoot, propelled forward by centrifugal force. Aft of Stores, I heard the whistle of escaping air and high pressure gasses from ruptured lines. Vapor clouds fogged the air. I called for floodlights for the whole sector.

Clay appeared out of the fog with his damage control crew. "Sir," he said, "it's punctured inner and outer shells in two places, and fragments have riddled the whole sector. There are at least three men dead, and two hurt."

"Taylor," I called, "let's have another damage control crew back here on the triple. Get the medics back here, too." Clay and his men put on masks and moved off. I borrowed one from a man standing by and followed.

The large exit puncture was in the forward cargo lock. The room was sealed off, limiting the air loss.

"Clay," I said, "pass this up for the moment and get that entry puncture sealed. I'll put the extra crew in suits to handle this."

I moved back into clear air and called for reports from all sections. The worst of the damage was in the auxiliary power control room, where communication and power lines were slashed and the panel cut up. The danger of serious damage to essential equipment had been very close, but we had been lucky. This was the first instance I had heard of encountering an object at hyper light speed.

It was astonishing how this threat to our safety cleared the air. The men went about their duties more cheerfully than they had for months, and Kramer was conspicuous by his subdued air. The emergency had reestablished at least for the time the normal discipline; the men still relied on the Captain in trouble.

Damage control crews worked steadily for the next seventy-two hours, replacing wiring, welding, and testing. Power Section jockeyed endlessly, correcting air motions. Meanwhile, I checked almost hourly with Survey Section, hoping for good news to consolidate the improved morale situation.

It was on Sunday morning, just after dawn relief that Lt. Taylor came up to the bridge looking sick.

"Sir," he said, "we took more damage than we knew with that meteor strike." He stopped and swallowed hard.

"What have you got, Lieutenant?" I said.

"We missed a piece. It must have gone off on a tangent through stores into the cooler. Clipped the coolant line, and let warm air in. All the fresh frozen stuff is contaminated and rotten." He gagged. "I got a whiff of it, sir. Excuse me." He rushed away.

This was calamity.

We didn't carry much in the way of fresh natural food; but what we had was vital. It was a bulky, delicate cargo to handle, but the chemists hadn't yet come up with synthetics to fill all the dietary needs of man. We could get by fine for a long time on vitamin tablets and concentrates; but there were nutritional elements that you couldn't get that way. Hydroponics didn't help; we had to have a few ounces of fresh meat and vegetables grown in sunlight every week, or start to die within months.

I knew that Kramer wouldn't let this chance pass. As Medical Officer he would be well within his rights in calling to my attention the fact that our health would soon begin to suffer. I felt sure he would do so as loudly and publicly as possible at the first opportunity.

My best move was to beat him to the punch by making a general announcement, giving the facts in the best possible light. That might take some of the sting out of anything Kramer said later.

I gave it to them, short and to the point. "Men, we've just suffered a serious loss. All the fresh frozen stores are gone. That doesn't mean we'll be going on short rations; there are plenty of concentrates and vitamins aboard. But it does mean we're going to be suffering from deficiencies in our diet.

"We didn't come out here on a pleasure cruise; we're on a mission that leaves no room for failure. This is just one more fact for us to face. Now let's get on with the job."

I walked into the wardroom, drew a cup of near-coffee, and sat down. The screen showed a beach with booming surf. The sound track picked up the crash and hiss of the breakers. Considering the red plague that now covered the scene, I thought it was a poor choice. I dialed for a high view of rolling farmland.

Mannion sat at a table across the room with Kirschenbaum. They were hunched over their cups, not talking. I wondered where they stood. Mannion, Communications Officer, was neurotic, but an old Armed Force man. Discipline meant a lot to him. Kirschenbaum, Power Chief, was a joker, with cold eyes, and smarter than he seemed. The question was whether he was smart enough to idealize the stupidity of retreat now.

Kramer walked in, not wasting any time. He saw me and came over. He stopped a few feet from the table, and said loudly, "Captain, I'd like to know your plans, now that the possibility of continuing is out."

I sipped my near-coffee and looked at the rolling farmland. I didn't answer him. If I could get him mad, I could take him at his game.

Kramer turned red. He didn't like being ignored. The two at the other table were watching.

"Captain," Kramer said loudly. "As Medical Officer I have to know what measures you're taking to protect the health of the men."

This was a little better. He was on the defensive now; explaining why he had a right to question his Commander. I wanted him a little hotter though.

I looked up at him. "Kramer," I said in a clear, not too loud voice, "you're on watch. I don't want to find you hanging around the wardroom making light chit-chat until you're properly relieved from duty." I went back to my near-coffee and the farmland. A river was in view now, and beyond it distant mountains.

Kramer was furious. "Joyce has relieved me, Captain," he said, controlling his voice with an effort. "I felt I'd better take this matter up with you as soon as possible, since it affects the health of every man aboard." He was trying to keep cool, in command of himself.

"I haven't authorized any changes in the duty roster, Major," I said mildly. "Report to your post." I was riding the habit of discipline now, as far as it would carry me. I hoped that disobedience to a direct order, solidly based on regulations, was a little too big a jump for Kramer at the moment. Tomorrow it might be different. But it was essential that I break up the scene he was staging.

He wilted. "I'll see you at 1700 in the chart room, Kramer," I said as he turned away. Mannion and Kirschenbaum looked at each other, then finished their near-coffee hurriedly and left. I hoped their version of the incident would help deflate Kramer's standing among the malcontents.

I left the wardroom and took the lift up to the bridge and checked with Clay and his survey team.

"I think I've spotted a slight perturbation in Delta 3, Captain," Clay said. "I'm not sure, we're still pretty far out."

"All right, Clay," I said. "Stay with it."

Clay was one of my more dependable men, dedicated to his work. Unfortunately, he was no man of action. He would have little influence in a show-down.

I was at the Schmidt when I heard the lift open. I turned; Kramer, Fine, Taylor, and a half a dozen enlisted crew chiefs crowded out, bunched together. They were all wearing needlers. At least they'd learned that much, I thought.

Kramer moved forward. "We feel that the question of the men's welfare has to be dealt with right away, Captain," he said smoothly.

I looked at him coldly, glanced at the rest of his crew. I said nothing.

"What we're faced with is pretty grim, even if we turn back now. I can't be responsible for the results if there's any delay," Kramer said. He spoke in an arrogant tone. I looked them over, let the silence build.

"You're in charge of this menagerie?" I said, looking at Kramer. "If so, you've got thirty seconds to send them back to their kennels. We'll go into the matter of unauthorized personnel on the bridge later. As for you, Major, you can consider yourself under arrest in quarters. Now Move."

Kramer was ready to stare me down, but Fine gave me a break by tugging at his sleeve. Kramer shook him loose, snarling. At that the crew chiefs faded back into the lift. Fine and Taylor hesitated, then joined them.

Kramer started to shout after them, then got hold of himself. The lift moved down.

Kramer thought about going for his needler. I looked at him through narrowed eyes. He decided to rely on his mouth, as usual. He licked his lips. "All right, I'm under arrest," he said. "But as Medical Officer of this vessel it's my duty to remind you that you can't live without a certain minimum of fresh organic food. We've got to start back now." He was pale, but determined. He couldn't bear the thought of getting bald and toothless from dietary deficiency. The girls would never give him another look.

"We're going on, Kramer," I said. "As long as we have a man aboard still able to move. Teeth or no teeth."

"Deficiency disease is no joke, Captain," Kramer said. "You can get all the symptoms of leprosy, cancer and syphilis just by skipping a few necessary elements in your diet. And we're missing most of them."

"Giving me your opinions is one thing, Kramer," I said. "Mutiny is another."

Clay stood beside the main screen, wide-eyed. I couldn't send Kramer down under his guard. "Let's go, Kramer," I said. "I'm locking you up myself."

We rode down in the lift. The men who had been with Kramer stood awkwardly, silent as we stepped out into the passage. I spotted two chronic trouble-makers among them. I thought I might as well call them now as later. "Williams and Nagle," I said, "this officer is under arrest. Escort him to his quarters and lock him in." As they stepped forward hesitantly, Kramer said, "Keep your filthy hooks off me." He started down the passage.

If I could get Kramer put away before anybody else started trouble, I might be able to bluff it through. I followed him and his two sheepish guards down past the power section, and the mess. I hoped there would be no crowd there to see their hero Kramer under guard.

I was out of luck. Apparently word had gone out of Kramer's arrest, and the corridor was clogged with men. They stood unmoving as we approached. Kramer stopped.

"Clear this passage, you men," I said.

Slowly they began to move back, giving ground reluctantly.

Suddenly Kramer shouted. "That's right, you whiners and complainers, clear the way so the Captain can take me back to the missile deck and shoot me. You just want to talk about home; you haven't got the guts to do anything about it."

The moving mass halted, milled. Someone shouted, "Who's he think he is, anyway."

Kramer whirled toward me. "He thinks he's the man who's going to let you all rot alive, to save his record."

"Williams, Nagle," I said loudly, "clear this passage."

Williams started half-heartedly to shove at the men nearest him. A fist flashed out and snapped his head back. That was a mistake; Williams pulled his needler, and fired a ricochet down the passage.

"'Bout twelve a you yellow-bellies git outa my way," he yelled. "I'm comin' through."

Nagle moved close to Williams, and shouted something to him. The noise drowned it. Kramer swung back to me, frantic to regain his sway over the mob.

"Once I'm out of the way, there'll be a general purge," he roared. The hubbub faded, as men turned to hear him.

"You're all marked men. He's gone mad. He won't let one of you live." Kramer had their eyes now. "Take him now," he shouted, and seized my arm to begin the action.

He'd rushed it a little. I hit him across the face with the back of my hand. No one jumped to his assistance. I drew my 2mm. "If you ever lay a hand on your Commanding Officer again, I'll burn you where you stand, Kramer."

Then a voice came from behind me. "You're not killing anybody without a trial, Captain." Joyce stood there with two of the crew chiefs, needler in hand. Fine and Taylor were not in sight.

I pushed Kramer out of my way and walked up to Joyce.

"Hand me that weapon, Junior, butt first," I said. I looked him in the eye with all the glare I had. He stepped back a pace.

"Why don't you jump him," he called to the crowd.

The wall annunciator hummed and spoke.

"Captain Greylorn, please report to the bridge. Unidentified body on main scope."

Every man stopped in his tracks, listening. The annunciator continued. "Looks like it's decelerating, Captain."

I holstered my pistol, pushed past Joyce, and trotted for the lift. The mob behind me broke up, talking, as men under long habit ran for action stations.

Clay was operating calmly under pressure. He sat at the main screen, and studied the blip, making tiny crayon marks.

"She's too far out for a reliable scanner track, Captain," he said, "but I'm pretty sure she's braking."

If that were true, this might be the break we'd been living for. Only manned or controlled bodies decelerated in deep space.

"How did you spot it, Clay?" I asked. Picking up a tiny mass like this was a delicate job, even when you knew its coordinates.

"Just happened to catch my eye, Captain," he said. "I always make a general check every watch of the whole forward quadrant. I noticed a blip where I didn't remember seeing one before."

"You have quite an eye, Clay," I said. "How about getting this object in the beam."

"We're trying now, Captain," he said. "That's a mighty small field, though."

Joyce called from the radar board, "I think I'm getting an echo at 15,000, sir. It's pretty weak."

Miller, quiet and meticulous, delicately tuned the beam control. "Give me your fix, Joyce," he said. "I can't find it."

Joyce called out his figures, in seconds of arc to three places.

"You're right on it, Joyce," Miller called a minute later. "I got it. Now pray it don't get away when I boost it."

Clay stepped over behind Miller. "Take it a few mags at a time," he said calmly.

I watched Miller's screen. A tiny point near the center of the screen swelled to a spec, and jumped nearly off the screen to the left. Miller centered it again, and switched to a higher power. This time it jumped less, and resolved into two tiny dots.

Step by step the magnification was increased as ring after ring of the lens antenna was thrown into play. Each time the centering operation was more delicate. The image grew until it filled a quarter of the screen. We stared at it in fascination.

It showed up in stark silhouette, in the electronic "light" of the radar scope. Two perfect discs, joined by a fine filament. As we watched, their relative positions slowly shifted, one moving across, half occluding the other.

As the image drifted, Miller worked with infinite care at his console to hold it on center, in sharp focus.

"Wish you'd give me an orbit on this thing, Joyce," he said, "so I could lock onto it."

"It ain't got no orbit, man," Joyce said. "I'm trackin' it, but I don't understand it. That rock is on a closing curve with us, and slowin' down fast."

"What's the velocity, Joyce?" I asked.

"Averagin' about 1,000 relative, Captain, but slowin' fast."

"All right, we'll hold our course," I said.

I keyed for a general announcement.

"This is the Captain," I said. "General Quarters. Man action stations and prepare for possible contact within one hour."

"Missile Section. Arm No. 1 Battery and stand by."

Then I added, "We don't know what we've got here, but it's not a natural body. Could be anything from a torpedo on up."

I went back to the Beam screen. The image was clear, but without detail. The two discs slowly drew apart, then closed again.

"I'd guess that movement is due to rotation of two spheres around a common center," Clay said.

"I agree with you," I said. "Try to get me a reading on the mass of the object."

I wondered whether Kramer had been locked up as I had ordered, but at this moment it seemed unimportant. If this was, as I hoped, a contact with our colony, all our troubles were over.

The object (I hesitated to call it a ship) approached steadily, still decelerating. Now Clay picked it up on the televideo, as it paralleled our course forty-five hundred miles out.

"Captain, it's my guess the body will match speeds with us at about 200 miles, at his present rate of deceleration," Clay said.

"Hold everything you've got on him, and watch closely for anything that might be a missile," I said.

Clay worked steadily over his chart table. Finally he turned to me. "Captain, I get a figure of over a hundred million tons mass; and calibrating the scope images gives us a length of nearly two miles."

I let that sink in. I had a strong and very empty feeling that this ship, if ship it were, was not an envoy from any human colony.

The annunciator hummed and spoke. "Captain, I'm getting a very short wave transmission from a point out on the starboard bow. Does that sound like your torpedo?" It was Mannion.

"That's it, Mannion," I said. "Can you make anything of it?"

"No, sir," he answered. "I'm taping it, so I can go to work on it."

Mannion was our language and code man. I hoped he was good.

"What does it sound like," I asked. "Tune me in."

After a moment a high hum came from the speaker. Through it I could hear harsh chopping consonants, a whining intonation. I doubted that Mannion would be able to make anything of that gargle.

Our Bogie closed steadily. At four hundred twenty-five miles he reversed relative directions, and began matching our speed, moving closer to our course. There was no doubt he planned to parallel us.

I made a brief announcement to all hands describing the status of the action. Clay worked over his televideo, trying to clear the image. I watched as the blob on the screen swelled and flickered. Suddenly it flashed into clear stark definition. Against a background of sparkling black, the twin spheres gleamed faintly in reflected starlight.

There were no visible surface features; the iodine-colored forms and their connecting shaft had an ancient and alien look.

We held our course steadily, watching the stranger maneuver. Even at this distance it looked huge.

"Captain," Clay said, "I've been making a few rough calculations. The two spheres are about 800 yards in diameter, and at the rate the structure is rotating it's pulling about six gravities."

That settled the question of human origin of the ship. No human crew would choose to work under six gee's.

Now, paralleling us at just over two hundred miles, the giant ship spun along, at rest relative to us. It was visible now through the direct observation panel, without magnification.

I left Clay in charge on the bridge, and I went down to the Com Section.

Joyce sat at his board, reading instruments and keying controls. So he was back on the job. Mannion sat, head bent, monitoring his recorder. The room was filled with the keening staccato of the alien transmission.

"Getting anything on video?" I asked. Joyce shook his head. "Nothing, Captain. I've checked the whole spectrum, and this is all I get. It's coming in on about a dozen different frequencies; no FM."

"Any progress, Mannion?" I said.

He took off his headset. "It's the same thing, repeated over and over, just a short phrase. I'd have better luck if they'd vary it a little."

"Try sending," I said.

Joyce tuned the clatter down to a faint clicking, and switched his transmitter on. "You're on, Captain," he said.

"This is Captain Greylorn, UNACV Galahad; kindly identify yourself." I repeated this slowly, half a dozen times. It occurred to me that this was the first known time in history a human being had addressed a non-human intelligence. The last was a guess, but I couldn't interpret our guest's purposeful maneuverings as other than intelligent.

I checked with the bridge; no change. Suddenly the clatter stopped, leaving only the carrier hum.

"Can't you tune that whine out, Joyce?" I asked.

"No, sir," he replied. "That's a very noisy transmission. Sounds like maybe their equipment is on the blink."

We listened to the hum, waiting. Then the clatter began again.

"This is different," Mannion said. "It's longer."

I went back to the bridge, and waited for the next move from the stranger, or for word from Mannion. Every half hour I transmitted a call identifying us, followed by a sample of our language. I gave them English, Russian, and Standard Interlingua. I didn't know why, but somehow I had a faint hope they might understand some of it.

I stayed on the bridge when the watch changed. I had some food sent up, and slept a few hours on the OD's bunk.

Fine replaced Kramer on his watch when it rolled around. Apparently Kramer was out of circulation. At this point I did not feel inclined to pursue the point.

We had been at General Quarters for twenty-one hours when the wall annunciator hummed.

"Captain, this is Mannion. I've busted it...."

"I'll be right there," I said, and left at a run.

Mannion was writing as I entered ComSection. He stopped his recorder and offered me a sheet. "This is what I've got so far, Captain," he said.

I read: INVADER; THE MANCJI PRESENCE OPENS COMMUNICATIONS.

"That's a highly inflected version of early Interlingua, Captain," Mannion said. "After I taped it, I compensated it to take out the rise-and-fall tone, and then filtered out the static. There were a few sound substitutions to figure out, but I finally caught on. It still doesn't make much sense, but that's what it says."

"I wonder what we're invading," I said. "And what is the "Mancji Presence'?"

"They just repeat that over and over," Mannion said. "They don't answer our call."

"Try translating into old Interlingua, adding their sound changes, and then feeding their own rise-and-fall routine to it," I said. "Maybe that will get a response."

I waited while Mannion worked out the message, then taped it on top of their whining tone pattern. "Put plenty of horse-power behind it," I said. "If their receivers are as shaky as their transmitter, they might not be hearing us."

We sent for five minutes, then tuned them back in and waited. There was a long silence from their side, then they came back with a long spluttering sing-song.

Mannion worked over it for several minutes. .ldThey must have understood us, here's what I get," he said:

THAT WHICH SWIMS IN THE MANCJI SEA; WE ARE AWARE THAT YOU HAVE THIS TRADE TONGUE. YOU RANGE FAR. IT IS OUR WHIM TO INDULGE YOU; WE ARE AMUSED THAT YOU PRESUME HERE; WE ACKNOWLEDGE YOUR INSOLENT DEMANDS.

"It looks like we're in somebody's back yard," I said. "They acknowledge our insolent demands, but they don't answer them." I thought a moment. "Send this," I said. "We'll out-strut them:"

THE MIGHTY WARSHIP GALAHAD REJECTS YOUR JURISDICTION.

TELL US THE NATURE OF YOUR DISTRESS AND WE MAY CHOOSE TO OFFER AID.

Mannion raised an eyebrow. "That ought to rock them," he said.

"They were eager to talk to us," I said. "That means they want something, in my opinion. And all the big talk sounds like a bluff of our own is our best line."

"Why do you want to antagonize them, Captain?" Joyce asked. "That ship is over a thousand times the size of this can."

"Joyce, I suggest you let me forget you're around," I said.

The Mancji whine was added to my message, and it went out. Moments later this came back:

MANCJI HONOR DICTATES YOUR SAFE-CONDUCT; TALK IS WEARYING; WE FIND IT CONVENIENT TO SOLICIT A TRANSFER OF ELECTROSTATIC FORCE.

"What the devil does that mean?" I said. "Tell them to loosen up and explain themselves."

Mannion wrote out a straight query, and sent it. Again we waited for a reply.

It came, in a long windy paragraph stating that the Mancji found electro-static baths amusing, and that "crystallization" had drained their tanks. They wanted a flow of electrons from us to replenish their supply.

"This sounds like simple electric current they're talking about, Captain," Mannion said. "They want a battery charge."

"They seem to have power to burn," I said. "Why don't they generate their own juice? Ask them; and find out where they learned Interlingua."

Mannion sent again; the reply was slow in coming back. Finally we got it:

THE MANCJI DO NOT EMPLOY MASSIVE GENERATION - PIECE WHERE ACCUMULATOR-PIECE IS SUFFICIENT. THIS SIMPLE TRADE SPEECH IS OF OLD KNOWLEDGE. WE SELECT IT FROM SYMBOLS WE ARE PLEASED TO SENSE EMPATTERNED ON YOUR HULL.

That made some sort of sense, but I was intrigued by the reference to Interlingua as a trade language. I wanted to know where they had learned it. I couldn't help the hope I started building on the idea that this giant knew our colony, in spite of the fact that they were using an antique version of the language, predating Omega by several centuries.

I sent another query, but the reply was abrupt and told nothing except that Interlingua was of "old knowledge."

Then Mannion entered a long technical exchange, getting the details of the kind of electric power they wanted.

"We can give them what they want, no sweat, Captain," he said after half an hour's talk. "They want DC; 100 volt, 50 amp will do."

"Ask them to describe themselves," I directed. I was beginning to get an idea.

Mannion sent, got his reply. "They're molluscoid, Captain," he said. He looked shocked. "They weigh about two tons each."

"Ask them what they eat," I said.

I turned to Joyce as Mannion worked over the message. "Get Kramer up here, on the double," I said.

Kramer came in five minutes later, looking drawn and rumpled. He stared at me sullenly.

"I'm releasing you from arrest temporarily on your own parole, Major," I said. "I want you to study the reply to our last transmission, and tell me what you can about it."

"Why me?" Kramer said. "I don't know what's going on." I didn't answer him.

There was a long tense half hour wait before Mannion copied out the reply that came in a stuttering nasal. He handed it to me.

As I had hoped, the message, after a preliminary recital of the indifference of the Mancji to biological processes of ingestion, recited a list of standard biochemical symbols.

"Can we eat this stuff?" I asked Kramer, handing him the sheet.

He studied it, and some of his accustomed swagger began to return. "I don't know what the flowery phrases are all about, but the symbols refer to common proteins, lipins, carbohydrates, vitamins, and biomins," he said. "What is this, a game?"

"All right, Mannion," I said. I was trying to hold back the excitement. "Ask them if they have fresh sources of these substances aboard."

The reply was quick; they did.

"Tell them we will exchange electric power for a supply of these foods. Tell them we want samples of half a dozen of the natural substances."

Again Mannion coded and sent, received and translated, sent again.

"They agree, Captain," he said at last. "They want us to fire a power lead out about a mile; they'll come in close and shoot us a specimen case with a flare on it. Then we can each check the other's merchandise."

"All right," I said. "We can use a ground-service cable; rig a pilot light on it, and kick it out, as soon as they get in close."

"We'll have to splice a couple of extra lengths to it," Mannion said.

"Go to it, Mannion," I said. "And send two of your men out to make the pick-up." This wasn't a communications job, but I wanted a reliable man handling it.

I returned to the bridge and keyed for Bourdon, directed him to arm two of his penetration missiles, lock them onto the stranger, and switch over to my control. With the firing key in my hand, I stood at the televideo screen and watched for any signs of treachery. The ship moved in, came to rest filling the screen.

Mannion's men reported out. I saw the red dot of our power lead move away, then a yellow point glowed on the side of the vast iodine-colored wall looming across the screen.

Nothing else emerged from the alien ship. The red pilot drifted across the face of the sphere. Mannion reported six thousand feet of cable out before the pilot disappeared abruptly.

"Captain," Mannion reported, "they're drawing power."

"O.K.," I said. "Let them have a sample, then shut down."

I waited, watching carefully, until Mannion reported the cannister inside.

"Kramer," I said. "Run me a fast check on the samples in that container."

Kramer was recovering his swagger. "You'll have to be a little more specific," he said. "Just what kind of analysis do you have in mind? Do you want a full...."

"I just want to know one thing, Kramer," I said. "Can we assimilate these substances, yes or no. If you don't feel like co-operating, I'll have you lashed to your bunk, and injected with them. You claim you're a medical officer; let's see you act like one." I turned my back to him.

Mannion called. "They say the juice we fed them was 'amusing,' Captain. I guess that means it's O.K."

"I'll let you know in a few minutes how their samples pan out," I said.

Kramer took half an hour before reporting back. "I ran a simple check such as I normally use in a routine mess inspection," he began. He couldn't help trying to take the center of the stage to go into his Wise Doctor and Helpless Patient routine.

"Yes or no," I said.

"Yes, we can assimilate most of it," he said angrily. "There were six samples. Two were gelatinous substances, non-nutritive. Three were vegetable-like, bulky and fibrous, one with a high iodine content; the other was a very normal meaty specimen."

"Which should we take?" I said. "Remember your teeth when you answer."

"The high protein, the meaty one," he said. "Marked '6'."

I keyed for Mannion. "Tell them that in return for 1,000 KWH we require 3,000 kilos of sample six," I said.

Mannion reported back. "They agreed in a hurry, Captain. They seem to feel pretty good about the deal. They want to chat, now that they've got a bargain. I'm still taping a long tirade."

"Good," I said. "Better get ready to send about six men with an auxiliary pusher to bring home the bacon. You can start feeding them the juice again."

I turned to Kramer. He was staring at the video image. "Report yourself back to arrest in quarters, Kramer," I said. "I'll take your services today into account at your court-martial."

Kramer looked up, with a nasty grin. "I don't know what kind of talking oysters you're trafficking with, but I'd laugh like hell if they vaporized your precious tub as soon as they're through with you." He walked out.

Mannion called in again from ComSection. "Here's their last, Captain," he said. "They say we're lucky they had a good supply of this protein aboard. It's one of their most amusing foods. It's a creature they discovered in the wild state and it's very rare. The wild ones have died out, and only their domesticated herds exist."

"O.K., we're lucky," I said. "It better be good or we'll step up the amperage and burn their batteries for them."

"Here's more," Mannion said. "They say it will take a few hours to prepare the cargo. They want us to be amused."

I didn't like the delay, but it would take us about 10 hours to deliver the juice to them at the trickle rate they wanted. Since the sample was O.K., I was assuming the rest would be too. We settled down to wait.

I left Clay in charge on the bridge and made a tour of the ship. The meeting with the alien had apparently driven the mood of mutiny into the background. The men were quiet and busy. I went to my cabin and slept for a few hours.

I was awakened by a call from Clay telling me that the alien had released his cargo for us. Mannion's crew was out making the pick-up. Before they had maneuvered the bulky cylinder to the cargo hatch, the alien released our power lead.

I called Kramer and told him to meet the incoming crew and open and inspect the cargo. If it was the same as the sample, I thought, we had made a terrific trade. Discipline would recover if the men felt we still had our luck.

Then Mannion called again. "Captain," he said excitedly, "I think there may be trouble coming. Will you come down, sir?"

"I'll go to the bridge, Mannion," I said. "Keep talking."

I tuned my speaker down low and listened to Mannion as I ran for the lift.

"They tell us to watch for a little display of Mancji power. They ran out some kind of antenna. I'm getting a loud static at the top of my short wave receptivity."

I ran the lift up and as I stepped onto the bridge I said, "Clay, stand by to fire."

As soon as the pick-up crew was reported in, I keyed course corrections to curve us off sharply from the alien. I didn't know what he had, but I liked the idea of putting space between us. My P-Missiles were still armed and locked.

Mannion called, "Captain, they say our fright is amusing, and quite justified."

I watched the televideo screen for the first sign of an attack. Suddenly the entire screen went white, then blanked. Miller, who had been at the scanner searching over the alien ship at close range, reeled out of his seat, clutching at his eyes. "My God, I'm blinded," he shouted.

Mannion called, "Captain, my receivers blew. I think every tube in the shack exploded!"

I jumped to the direct viewer. The alien hung there, turning away from us in a leisurely curve. There was no sign of whatever had blown us off the air. I held my key, but didn't press it. I told Clay to take Miller down to Medic. He was moaning and in severe pain.

Kramer reported in from the cargo deck. The cannister was inside now, coating up with frost. I told him to wait, then sent Chilcote, my demolition man, in to open it. Maybe it was booby-trapped. I stood by at the DVP and waited for other signs of Mancjo power to hit us. The general feeling was tense.

Apparently they were satisfied with one blast of whatever it was; they were dwindling away with no further signs of life.

After half an hour of tense alertness, I ordered the missiles disarmed.

I keyed for General. "Men, this is the Captain," I said. "It looks as though our first contact with an alien race has been successfully completed. He is now at a distance of three hundred and moving off fast. Our screens are blown, but there's no real damage. And we have a supply of fresh food aboard; now let's get back to business. That colony can't be far off."

That may have been rushing it some, but if the food supply we'd gotten was a dud, we were finished anyway.

We watched the direct-view screen till the ship was lost; then followed on radar.

"It's moving right along, Captain," Joyce said, "accelerating at about two gee's."

"Good riddance," Clay said. "I don't like dealing with armed maniacs."

"They were screwballs all right," I said, "but they couldn't have happened along at a better time. I only wish we had been in a position to squeeze a few answers out of them."

"Yes, sir," Clay said. "Now that the whole thing's over, I'm beginning to think of a lot of questions myself."

The annunciator hummed. I heard what sounded like hoarse breathing. I glanced at the indicator light. It was the cargo deck mike that was open.

I keyed. "If you have a report, Chilcote, go ahead," I said.

Suddenly someone was shouting into the mike, incoherently. I caught words, cursing. Then Chilcote's voice, "Captain," he said. "Captain, please come quick." There was a loud clatter, noise, then only the hum of the mike.

"Take over, Clay," I said, and started back to the cargo deck at a dead run.

Men crowded the corridor, asking questions, milling. I forced my way through, found Kramer surrounded by men, shouting.

"Break this up," I shouted. "Kramer, what's your report?"

Chilcote walked past me, pale as chalk. I pushed through to Kramer.

"Get hold of yourself, and make your report, Kramer," I said. "What started this riot?"

Kramer stopped shouting, and stood looking at me, panting. The crowded men fell silent.

"I gave you a job to do, Major," I said; "opening a cargo can. Now you take it from there."

"Yeah, Captain," he said. "We got it open. No wires, no traps. We hauled the load out of the can on to the floor. It was one big frozen mass, wrapped up in some kind of netting. Then we pulled the covering off."

"All right, go ahead," I said.

"That load of fresh meat your star-born pals gave us consists of about six families of human beings; men, women, and children." Kramer was talking for the crowd now, shouting. "Those last should be pretty tender when you ration out our ounce a week, Captain."

The men milled, wide-eyed, open-mouthed, as I thrust through to the cargo lock. The door stood ajar and wisps of white vapor curled out into the passage.

I stepped through the door. It was bitter cold in the lock. Near the outer hatch the bulky cannister, rimed with white frost, lay in a pool of melting ice. Before it lay the half shrouded bulk that it had contained. I walked closer.

They were frozen together into one solid mass. Kramer was right. They were as human as I. Human corpses, stripped, packed together, frozen. I pulled back the lightly frosted covering, and studied the glazed white bodies.

Kramer called suddenly from the door. "You found your colonists, Captain. Now that your curiosity is satisfied, we can go back where we belong. Out here man is a tame variety of cattle. We're lucky they didn't know we were the same variety, or we'd be in their food lockers now ourselves. Now let's get started back. The men won't take 'no' for an answer."

I leaned closer, studying the corpses. "Come here, Kramer," I called. "I want to show you something."

"I've seen all there is to see in there," Kramer said. "We don't want to waste time; we want to change course now, right away."

I walked back to the door, and as Kramer stepped back to let me precede him out the door, I hit him in the mouth with all my strength. His head snapped back against the frosted wall. Then he fell out into the passage.

I stepped over him. "Pick this up and put it in the brig," I said. The men in the corridor fell back, muttering. As they hauled Kramer upright I stepped through them and kept going, not running but wasting no time, toward the bridge. One wrong move on my part now and all their misery and fear would break loose in a riot the first act of which would be to tear me limb from limb.

I travelled ahead of the shock. Kramer had provided the diversion I had needed. Now I heard the sound of gathering violence growing behind me.

I was none too quick. A needler flashed at the end of the corridor just as the lift door closed. I heard the tiny projectile ricochet off the lift shaft.

I rode up, stepped onto the bridge and locked the lift. I keyed for Bourdon, and to my relief got a quick response. The panic hadn't penetrated to Missile Section yet.

"Bourdon, arm all batteries and lock onto that Mancji ship," I ordered. "On the triple."

I turned to Clay. "I'll take over, Clay," I said. "Alter course to intercept our late companion at two and one-half gee's."

Clay looked startled, but said only, "Aye, sir."

I keyed for a general announcement. "This is the Captain," I said. "Action station, all hands in loose acceleration harness. We're going after Big Brother. You're in action against the enemy now, and from this point on I'm remembering. You men have been having a big time letting off steam; that's over now. All sections report."

One by one the sections reported in, all but Med. and Admin. Well, I could spare them for the present. The pressure was building now, as we blasted around in a hairpin curve, our acceleration picking up fast.

I ordered Joyce to lock his radar on target, and switch over to autopilot control. Then I called Power Section.

"I'm taking over all power control from the bridge," I said. "All personnel out of the power chamber and control chamber."

The men were still under control, but that might not last long. I had to have the entire disposition of the ship's power, control, and armament under my personal direction for a few hours at least.

Missile Section reported all missiles armed and locked on target. I acknowledged and ordered the section evacuated. Then I turned to Clay and Joyce. Both were plenty nervous now; they didn't know what was brewing.

"Lieutenant Clay," I said. "Report to your quarters; Joyce, you too. I want to congratulate both of you on a soldierly performance these last few hours."

They left without protest. I was aware that they didn't want to be too closely identified with the Captain when things broke loose.

I keyed for a video check of the interior of the lift as it started back up. It was empty. I locked it up.

Now we were steady on course, and had reached our full two and a half gees. I could hardly stand under that acceleration, but I had one more job to do before I could take a break.

Feet dragging, I unlocked the lift and rode it down. I was braced for violence as I opened the lift door, but I was lucky. There was no one in the corridor. I could hear shouts in the distance. I dragged myself along to Power Section and pushed inside. A quick check of control settings showed everything as I had ordered it. Back in the passage, I slammed the leaded vault door to and threw in the combination lock. Now only I could open it without blasting.

Control Section was next. It, too, was empty, all in order. I locked it, and started across to Missiles. Two men appeared at the end of the passage, having as hard a time as I was. I entered the cross corridor just in time to escape a volley of needler shots. The mutiny was in the open now, for sure.

I kept going, hearing more shouting. I was sure the men I had seen were heading for Power and Control. They'd get a surprise. I hoped I could beat them to the draw at Missiles, too.

As I came out in B corridor, twenty feet from Missiles, I saw that I had cut it a bit fine. Three men, crawling, were frantically striving against the multi-gee field to reach the door before me. Their faces were running with sweat, purple with exertion.

I had a slight lead; it was too late to make a check inside before locking up. The best I could hope for was to lock the door before they reached it.

I drew my Browning and started for the door. They saw me and one reached for his needler.

"Don't try it," I called. I concentrated on the door, reached it, swung it closed, and as I threw in the lock a needler cracked. I whirled and fired. The man in the rear had stopped and aimed as the other two came on. He folded. The other two kept coming.

I was tired. I wanted a rest. "You're too late," I said. "No one but the Captain goes in there now." I stopped talking, panting. I had to rest. The two came on. I wondered why they struggled so desperately after they were beaten. My thinking was slowing down.

I suddenly realized they might be holding me for the crowd to arrive. I shuffled backwards towards the cross corridor. I barely made it. Two men on a shuttle cart whirled around the corner a hundred feet aft. I lurched into my shelter in a hail of needler fire. One of the tiny slugs stung through my calf and ricocheted down the passage.

I called to the two I had raced; "Tell your boys if they ever want to open that door, just see the Captain."

I hesitated, considering whether or not to make a general statement.

"What the hell," I decided. "They all know there's a mutiny now. It won't hurt to get in a little life-insurance."

I keyed my mike. "This is the Captain," I said. "This ship is now in a state of mutiny. I call on all loyal members of the Armed Forces to resist the mutineers actively, and to support their Commander. Your ship is in action against an armed enemy. I assure you this mutiny will fail, and those who took part in it will be treated as traitors to their Service, their homes, and their own families who now rely on them.

"We are accelerating at two and one-half gravities, locked on a collision course with the Mancji ship. The mutineers cannot enter the Bridge, Power, Control, or

Missiles Sections since only I have the combination. Thus they're doomed to failure.

"I am now returning to the Bridge to direct the attack and destruction of the enemy. If I fail to reach the Bridge, we will collide with the enemy in less than three hours, and our batteries will blow."

Now my problem was to make good my remark about returning to the Bridge. The shuttle had not followed me, presumably fearing ambush. I took advantage of their hesitation to cross back to corridor A at my best speed. I paused once to send a hail of needles ricocheting down the corridor behind me, and I heard a yelp from around the corner. Those needles had a fantastic velocity, and bounced around a long time before stopping.

At the corridor, I lay down on the floor for a rest and risked a quick look. A group of three men were bunched around the Control Section door, packing smashite in the hairline crack around it. That wouldn't do them any good, but it did occupy their attention.

I faded back into the cross passage, and keyed the mike. I had to give them a chance.

"This is the Captain," I said. "All personnel not at their action stations are warned for the last time to report there immediately. Any man found away from his post from this point on is in open mutiny and can expect the death penalty. This is the last warning."

The men in the corridor had heard, but a glance showed they paid no attention to what they considered an idle threat. They didn't know how near I was.

I drew my needler, set it for continuous fire, pushed into the corridor, aimed, and fired. I shot to kill. All three sprawled away from the door, riddled, as the metal walls rang with the cloud of needles.

I looked both ways, then rose, with effort, and went to the bodies. I recognized them as members of Kirschenbaum's Power Section crew. I keyed again as I moved on toward the lift at the end of the corridor, glancing back as I went.

"Corley, Mac Williams, and Reardon have been shot for mutiny in the face of the enemy," I said. "Let's hope they're the last to insist on my enforcing the death penalty."

Behind me, at the far end of the corridor, men appeared again. I flattened myself in a doorway, sprayed needles toward them, and hoped for the best. I heard the singing of a swarm past me, but felt no hits. The mutineers offered a bigger target, and I thought I saw someone fall. As they all moved back out of sight, I made another break for the lift.

I was grateful they hadn't had time to organize. I kept an eye to the rear, and sent a hail of needles back every time a man showed himself. They ducked out to fire every few seconds, but not very effectively. I had an advantage over them; I was fighting for the success of the mission and for my life, with no one to look to for help; they were each one of a mob, none eager to be a target, each willing to let the other man take the risk.

I was getting pretty tired. I was grateful for the extra stamina and wind that daily calisthenics in a high-gee field had given me; without that I would have collapsed before now; but I was almost ready to drop. I had my eyes fixed on the lift door; each step, inch by inch, was an almost unbearable effort. With only a few feet to go, my knees gave; I went down on all fours. Another batch of needles sang around me, and vivid pain seared my left arm. It helped. The pain cleared my head, spurred me. I rose and stumbled against the door.

Now the combination. I fought a numbing desire to faint as I pressed the lock control; three, five, two, five...

I twisted around as I heard a sound. The shuttle was coming toward me, men lying flat on it, protected by the bumper plate. I leaned against the lift door, and loosed a stream of needles against the side of the corridor, banking them toward the shuttle. Two men rolled off the shuttle in a spatter of blood. Another screamed, and a hand waved above the bumper. I needled it.

I wondered how many were on the shuttle. It kept coming. The closer it came, the more effective my bank shots were. I wondered why it failed to return my fire. Then a hand rose in an arc and a choke bomb dropped in a short curve to the floor. It rolled to my feet, just starting to spew. I kicked it back. The shuttle stopped, backed away from the bomb. A jet of brown gas was playing from it now. I aimed my needler, and sent it spinning back farther. Then I turned to my lock.

Now a clank of metal against metal sounded behind me; from the side passage a figure in radiation armor moved out. The suit was self-powered and needle proof. I sent a concentrated blast at the head, as the figure awkwardly tottered toward me, ungainly in the multi-gee field. The needles hit, snapped the head back. The suited figure hesitated, arms spread, stepped back and fell with a thunderous crash. I had managed to knock him off balance, maybe stun him.

I struggled to remember where I was in the code sequence; I went on, keyed the rest. I pushed; nothing. I must have lost count. I started again.

I heard the armored man coming on again. The needler trick wouldn't work twice. I kept working. I had almost completed the sequence when I felt the powered grip of the suited man on my arm. I twisted, jammed the needler against his hand, and fired. The arm flew back, and even through the suit I heard his wrist snap. My own hand was numb from the recoil. The other arm of the suit swept down and struck my wounded arm. I staggered away from the door, dazed with the pain.

I side-stepped in time to miss another ponderous blow. Under two and a half gees, the man in the suit was having a hard time, even with power assisted controls. I felt that I was fighting a machine instead of a man.

As he stepped toward me again, I aimed at his foot. A concentrated stream of needles hit, like a metallic fire hose, knocked the foot aside, toppled the man again. I staggered back to my door.

But now I realized I couldn't risk opening it; even if I got in, I couldn't keep my suited assailant from crowding in with me. Already he was up, lurching toward me. I had to draw him away from the door.

The shuttle sat unmoving. The mob kept its distance. I wondered why no one was shooting; I guessed they had realized that if I were killed there would be no way to enter the vital control areas of the ship; they had to take me alive.

I made it past the clumsy armored man and started down the corridor toward the shuttle. I moved as slowly as I could while still eluding him. He lumbered after me. I reached the shuttle; a glance showed no one alive there. Two men lay across it. I pulled myself onto it and threw in the forward lever. The shuttle rolled smoothly past the armored man, striking him a glancing blow that sent him down again. Those falls, in the multi-gee field, were bone crushing. He didn't get up.

I reached the door again, rolled off the shuttle, and reached for the combination. I wished now I'd used a shorter one. I started again; heard a noise behind me. As I turned, a heavy weight crushed me against the door.

I was held rigid, my chest against the combination key. The pressure was cracking my ribs and still it increased. I twisted my head, gasping. The shuttle held me pinned to the door. The man I had assumed out of action was alive enough to hold the lever down with savage strength. I tried to shout, to remind him that without me to open the doors, they were powerless to save the ship. I couldn't speak. I tasted blood in my mouth, and tried to breathe. I couldn't. I passed out.

Chapter 2

I emerged into consciousness to find the pressure gone, but a red haze of pain remained. I lay on my back and saw men sitting on the floor around me.

A blow from somewhere made my head ring. I tried to sit up. I couldn't make it. Then Kramer was beside me, slipping a needle into my arm. He looked pretty bad himself. His face was bandaged heavily, and one eye was purple. He spoke in a muffled voice through stiff jaws. His tone was deliberate.

"This will keep you conscious enough to answer a few questions," he said. "Now you're going to give me the combinations to the locks so we can call off this suicide run; then maybe I'll doctor you up."

I didn't answer.

"The time for clamming up is over, you stupid braggard," Kramer said. He raised his fist and drove a hard punch into my chest. I guess it was his shot that kept me conscious. I couldn't breathe for a while, until Kramer gave me a few whiffs of oxygen. I wondered if he was fool enough to think I might give up my ship.

After a while my head cleared a little. I tried to say something. I got out a couple of croaks, and then found my voice.

"Kramer," I said.

He leaned over me. "I'm listening," he said.

"Take me to the lift. Leave me there alone. That's your only chance." It seemed to me like a long speech, but nothing happened. Kramer went away, came back. He showed me a large scalpel from his medical kit. "I'm going to start operating on your face. I'll make you into a museum freak. Maybe if you start talking soon enough I'll change my mind."

I could see the watch on his wrist. My mind worked very slowly. I had trouble getting any air into my lungs. We would intercept in one hour and ten minutes.

It seemed simple to me. I had to get back to the Bridge before we hit. I tried again. "We only have an hour," I said.

Kramer lost control. He jabbed the knife at my face, screeching through gritted teeth. I jerked my head aside far enough that the scalpel grated along my cheekbone instead of slashing my mouth. I hardly felt it.

"We're not dying because you were a fool," Kramer yelled. "I've taken over; I've relieved you as unfit for command. Now open up this ship or I'll slice you to ribbons." He held the scalpel under my nose in a fist trembling with fury. The chrome plated blade had a thin film of pink on it.

I got my voice going again. "I'm going to destroy the Mancji ship," I said. "Take me to the lift and leave me there." I tried to add a few words, but had to stop and work on breathing again for a while. Kramer disappeared.

I realized I was not fully in command of my senses. I was clamped in a padded claw. I wanted to roll over. I tried hard, and made it. I could hear Kramer talking, others answering, but it seemed too great an effort to listen to the words.

I was lying on my face now, head almost against the wall. There was a black line in front of me, a door. My head cleared a bit. It must have been Kramer's shot working on me. I turned my head and saw Kramer standing now with half a dozen others, all talking at once. Apparently Kramer's display of uncontrolled temper had the others worried. They wanted me alive. Kramer didn't like anyone criticizing him. The argument was pretty violent. There was scuffling—and shouts.

I saw that I lay about twenty feet from the lift; too far. The door before me, if I remembered the ship's layout, was a utility room, small and containing nothing but a waste disposal hopper. But it did have a bolt on the inside, like every other room on the ship.

I didn't stop to think about it; I started trying to get up. If I'd thought I would have known that at the first move from me all seven of them would land on me at once. I concentrated on getting my hands under me, to push up. I heard a shout, and turning my head, saw Kramer swinging at someone. I went on with my project.

Hands under my chest, I raised myself a little, and got a knee up. I felt broken rib ends grating, but felt no pain, just the padded claw. Then I was weaving on all fours. I looked up, spotted the latch on the door, and put everything I had into lunging at it. My finger hit it, the door swung in, and I fell on my face; but I was half in. Another lunge and I was past the door, kicking it shut as I lay on the floor, reaching for the lock control.

Just as I flipped it with an extended finger, someone hit the door from outside, a second too late.

It was dark, and I lay on my back on the floor, and felt strange short-circuited stabs of what would have been agonizing pain running through my chest and arm. I had a few minutes to rest now, before they blasted the door open.

I hated to lose like this, not because we were beaten, but because we were giving up. My poor world, no longer fair and green, had found the strength to send us out as her last hope. But somewhere out here in the loneliness and distance we had lost our courage. Success was at our fingertips, if we could have found it; instead, in panic and madness, we were destroying ourselves.

My mind wandered; I imagined myself on the Bridge, half-believed I was there. I was resting on the OD bunk, and Clay was standing beside me. A long time seemed to pass.... Then I remembered I was on the floor, bleeding internally, in a tiny room that would soon lose its door. But there was someone standing beside me.

I didn't feel too disappointed at being beaten; I hadn't hoped for much more than a breather, anyway. I wondered why this fellow had abandoned his action station to hide there. The door was still shut. He must have been there all along, but I hadn't seen him when I came in. He stood over me, wearing greasy overalls, and grinned down at me. He raised his hand. I was getting pretty indifferent to blows; I couldn't feel them.

The hand went up, the man straightened and held a fairly snappy salute. "Sir," he said. "Space'n first class Thomas."

I didn't feel like laughing or cheering or anything else; I just took it as it came.

"At ease, Thomas," I managed to say. "Why aren't you at your duty station?" I went spinning off somewhere after that oration.

Thomas was squatting beside me now. "Cap'n, you're hurt, ain't you? I was wonderin' why you was down here layin down in my 'Sposal station."

"A scratch," I said. I thought about it for a while. Thomas was doing something about my chest. This was Thomas' disposal station. Thomas owned it. I wondered if a fellow could make a living with such a small place way out here, with just an occasional tourist coming by. I wondered why I didn't send one of them for help; I needed help for some reason....

"Cap'n, I been overhaulin' my converter units, I jist come in. How long you been in here, Cap'n?" Thomas was worried about something.

I tried hard to think. I hadn't been here very long; just a few minutes. I had come here to rest.... Then suddenly I was thinking clearly again.

Whatever Thomas was, he was apparently on my side, or at least neutral. He didn't seem to be aware of the mutiny. I realized that he had bound my chest tightly with strips of shirt; it felt better.

"What are you doing in here, Thomas?" I asked. "Don't you know we're in action against a hostile ship?"

Thomas looked surprised. "This here's my action station, Cap'n," he said. "I'm a Waste Recovery Technician, First Class, I keep the recovery system operatin'."

"You just stay in here?" I asked.

"No, sir," Thomas said. "I check through the whole system. We got three main disposal points and lots a little ones, an' I have to keep everything operatin'. Otherwise this ship would be in a bad way, Cap'n."

"How did you get in here?" I asked. I looked around the small room. There was only one door, and the gray bulk of the converter unit which broke down wastes into their component elements for re-use nearly filled the tiny space.

"I come in through the duct, Cap'n," Thomas said. "I check the ducts every day. You know, Cap'n," he said shaking his head, "they's some bad laid-out ductin' in this here system. If I didn't keep after it, you'd be gettin' clogged ducts all the time. So I jist go through the system and keep her clear."

From somewhere, hope began again. "Where do these ducts lead?" I asked. I wondered how the man could ignore the mutiny going on around him.

"Well, sir, one leads to the mess; that's the big one. One leads to the wardroom, and the other one leads up to the Bridge."

My God, I thought, the Bridge.

"How big are they?" I asked. "Could I get through them?"

"Oh, sure, Cap'n," Thomas said. "You can get through 'em easy. But are you sure you feel like inspectin' with them busted ribs?"

I was beginning to realize that Thomas was not precisely a genius. "I can make it," I said.

"Cap'n," Thomas said diffidently, "it ain't none a my business, but don't you think maybe I better get the doctor for ya?"

"Thomas," I said, "maybe you don't know; there's a mutiny under way aboard this ship. The doctor is leading it. I want to get to the Bridge in the worst way. Let's get started."

Thomas looked very shocked. "Cap'n, you mean you was hurt by somebody? I mean you didn't have a fall or nothin', you was beat up?" He stared at me with an expression of incredulous horror.

"That's about the size of it," I said. I managed to sit up. Thomas jumped forward and helped me to my feet. Then I saw that he was crying.

"You can count on me, Cap'n," he said. "Jist lemme know who done it, an' I'll feed 'em into my converter."

I stood leaning against the wall, waiting for my head to stop spinning. Breathing was difficult, but if I kept it shallow, I could manage. Thomas was opening a panel on the side of the converter unit.

"It's O.K. to go in Cap'n," he said. "She ain't operatin'."

The pull of the two and a half gees seemed to bother him very little. I could barely stand under it, holding on. Thomas saw my wavering step and jumped to help me. He boosted me into the chamber of the converter and pointed out an opening near the top, about twelve by twenty-four inches.

"That there one is to the Bridge, Cap'n," he said. "If you'll start in there, sir, I'll follow up."

I thrust head and shoulders into the opening. Inside it was smooth metal, with no handholds. I clawed at it trying to get farther in. The pain stabbed at my chest.

"Cap'n, they're workin' on the door," Thomas said. "They already been at it for a little while. We better get goin'."

"You'd better give me a push, Thomas," I said. My voice echoed hollowly down the duct.

Thomas crowded into the chamber behind me then, lifting my legs and pushing. I eased into the duct. The pain was not so bad now.

"Cap'n, you gotta use a special kinda crawl to get through these here ducts," Thomas said. "You grip your hands together out in front of ya, and then bend your elbows. When your elbows jam against the side of the duct, you pull forward."

I tried it; it was slow, but it worked.

"Cap'n," Thomas said behind me. "We got about seven minutes now to get up there. I set the control on the converter to start up in ten minutes. I think we can make it O.K., and ain't nobody else comin' this way with the converter goin'. I locked the control panel so they can't shut her down."

That news spurred me on. With the converter in operation, the first step in the cycle was the evacuation of the ducts to a near-perfect vacuum. When that happened, we would die instantly with ruptured lungs; then our dead bodies would be sucked into the chamber and broken down into useful raw materials. I hurried.

I tried to orient myself. The duct paralleled the corridor. It would continue in that direction for about fifteen feet, and would then turn upward, since the Bridge was some fifteen feet above this level. I hitched along, and felt the duct begin to trend upward.

"You'll have to get on your back here, Cap'n," Thomas said. "She widens out on the turn."

I managed to twist over. Thomas was helping me by pushing at my feet. As I reached a near-vertical position, I felt a metal rod under my hand. That was a relief; I had been expecting to have to go up the last stretch the way a mountain climber does a rock chimney, back against one wall and feet against the other.

I hauled at the rod, and found another with my other hand. Below, Thomas boosted me. I groped up and got another, then another. The remaining slight slant of the duct helped. Finally my feet were on the rods. I clung, panting. The heat in the duct was terrific. Then I went on up. That was some shot Kramer had given me.

Above I could see the end of the duct faintly in the light coming up through the open chamber door from the utility room. I remembered the location of the disposal slot on the Bridge now; it had been installed in the small apartment containing a bunk and a tiny galley for the use of the Duty Officer during long watches on the Bridge.

I reached the top of the duct and pushed against the slot cover. It swung out easily. I could see the end of the chart table, and beyond, the dead radar screen. I reached through and heaved myself partly out. I nearly fainted at the stab from my ribs as my weight went on my chest. My head sang. The light from below suddenly went out. I heard a muffled clank; then a hum began, echoing up the duct.

"She's closed and started cyclin' the air out, Cap'n," Thomas said calmly. "We got about half a minute."

I clamped my teeth together and heaved again. Below me Thomas waited quietly. He couldn't help me now. I got my hands flat against the bulkhead and thrust. The air was whistling around my face. Papers began to swirl off the chart table. I twisted my body frantically, kicking loose from the grip of the slot, fighting the sucking pull of air. I fell to the floor inside the room, the slot cover slamming behind me. I staggered to my feet. I pried at the cover, but I couldn't open it against the vacuum. Then it budged, and Thomas' hand came through. The metal edge cut into it, blood started, but the cover was held open half an inch. I reached the chart table, almost falling over my leaden feet, seized a short permal T-square, and levered the cover up. Once started, it went up easily. Thomas face appeared, drawn and pale, eyes closed against the dust being whirled into his face. He got his arms through, heaved himself a little higher. I seized his arm and pulled. He scrambled through.

I knocked the T-square out of the way and the cover snapped down. Then I slid to the floor, not exactly out, but needing a break pretty bad. Thomas brought bedding from the OD bunk and made me comfortable on the floor.

"Thomas," I said, "when I think of what the security inspectors who approved the plans for this arrangement are going to say when I call this little back door to their attention, it almost makes it worth the trouble."

"Yes, sir," Thomas said. He sprawled on the deck and looked around the Bridge, staring at the unfamiliar screens, indicator dials, controls.

From where I lay, I could see the direct vision screen. I wasn't sure, but I thought the small bright object in the center of it might be our target. Thomas looked at the dead radar screen, then said, "Cap'n, that there radarscope out of action?"

"It sure is, Thomas," I said. "Our unknown friends blew the works before they left us." I was surprised that he recognized a radarscope.

"Mind if I take a look at it, Cap'n?" he said.

"Go ahead," I replied. I tried to explain the situation to Thomas. The elapsed time since we had started our pursuit was two hours and ten minutes; I wanted to close to no more than a twenty mile gap before launching my missiles; and I had better alert my interceptor missiles in case the Mancji hit first.

Thomas had the cover off the radar panel and was probing around. He pulled a blackened card out of the interior of the panel.

"Looks like they overloaded the fuse," Thomas said. "Got any spares, Cap'n?"

"Right beside you in the cabinet," I said. "How do you know your way around a radar set, Thomas?"

Thomas grinned. "I useta be a radar technician third before I got inta waste disposal," he said. "I had to change specialities to sign on for this cruise."

I had an idea there'd be an opening for Thomas a little higher up when this was over.

I asked him to take a look at the televideo, too. I was beginning to realize that Thomas was not really simple; he was merely uncomplicated.

"Tubes blowed here, Cap'n," he reported. "Like as if you was to set her up to high mag right near a sun; she was overloaded. I can fix her easy if we got the spares."

I didn't take time to try to figure that one out. I could feel the dizziness coming on again.

"Thomas," I called, "let me know when we're at twenty miles from target." I wanted to tell him more, but I could feel consciousness draining away. "Then ..." I managed, "first aid kit ... shot...."

I could still hear Thomas. I was flying away, whirling, but I could hear his voice. "Cap'n, I could fire your missiles now, if you was to want me to," he was saying. I struggled to speak. "No. Wait." I hoped he heard me.

I floated a long time in a strange state between coma and consciousness. The stuff Kramer had given me was potent. It kept my mind fairly clear even when my senses were out of action. I thought about the situation aboard my ship.

I wondered what Kramer and his men were planning now, how they felt about having let me slip through their fingers. The only thing they could try now was blasting their way into the Bridge. They'd never make it. The designers of these ships were not unaware of the hazards of space life; the Bridge was an unassailable fortress. They couldn't possibly get to it.

I guessed that Kramer was having a pretty rough time of it now. He had convinced the men that we were rushing headlong to sure destruction at the hands of the all-powerful Mancji, and that their Captain was a fool. Now he was trapped with them in the panic he had helped to create. I thought that in all probability they had torn him apart.

I wavered in and out of consciousness. It was just as well; I needed the rest. Then I heard Thomas calling me. "We're closin' now, Cap'n," he said. "Wake up, Cap'n, only twenty-three miles now."

"Okay," I said. My body had been preparing itself for this, now it was ready again. I felt the needle in my arm. That helped, too.

"Hand me the intercom, Thomas," I said. He placed the mike in my hand. I keyed for a general announcement.

"This is the Captain," I said. I tried to keep my voice as steady as possible. "We are now at a distance of twenty-one miles from the enemy. Stand by for missile launching and possible evasive action. Damage control crews on the alert." I paused for breath.

"Now we're going to take out the Mancji ship, men," I said. "All two miles of it."

I dropped the mike and groped for the firing key. Thomas handed it to me.

"Cap'n," he said, bending over me. "I notice you got the selector set for your chemical warheads. You wouldn't want me to set up pluto heads for ya, would ya, Cap'n?"

"No, thanks, Thomas," I said. "Chemical is what I want. Stand by to observe." I pressed the firing key.

Thomas was at the radarscope. "Missiles away, Cap'n. Trackin' O.K. Looks like they'll take out the left half a that dumbbell."

I found the mike again. "Missiles homing on target," I said. "Strike in thirty-five seconds. You'll be interested to know we're employing chemical warheads. So far there is no sign of offense or defense from the enemy."

I figured the news would shock a few mutineers. David wasn't even using his slingshot on Goliath. He was going after him bare-handed. I wanted to scare some kind of response out of them. I needed a few clues as to what was going on below.

I got it. Joyce's voice came from the wall annunciator. "Captain, this is Lt. Joyce reporting." He sounded scared all the way through, and desperate. "Sir, the mutiny has been successfully suppressed by the loyal members of the crew. Major Kramer is under arrest. We're prepared to go on with the search for the Omega Colony. But Sir ..." he paused, gulping. "We ask you to change course now before launching any effective attack. We still have a chance. Maybe they won't bother with us when those firecrackers go off ..."

I watched the direct vision screen. Zero second closed in. And on the screen the face of the left hand disk of the Mancji ship was lit momentarily by a brilliant spark of yellow, then another. A discoloration showed dimly against the dark metallic surface. It spread, and a faint vapor formed over it. Now tiny specs could be seen moving away from the ship. The disk elongated, with infinite leisure, widening.

"What's happenin'? Cap'n?" Thomas asked. He was staring at the scope in fascination. "They launchin' scouts, or what?"

"Take a look here, Thomas," I said. "The ship is breaking up."

The disk was an impossibly long ellipse now, surrounded by a vast array of smaller bodies, fragments and contents of the ship. Now the stricken globe moved completely free of its companion. It rotated, presenting a crescent toward us, then wheeled farther as it receded from its twin, showing its elongation. The sphere had split wide open. Now the shattered half itself separated into two halves, and these in turn crumbled, strewing debris in a widening spiral.

"My God, Cap'n," Thomas said in awe. "That's the greatest display I ever seen. And all it took to set her off was 200 kilos a PBL. Now that's somethin'."

I keyed the mike again. "This is the Captain," I said. "I want ten four-man patrols ready to go out in fifteen minutes. The enemy ship has been put out of action and is now in a derelict condition. I want only one thing from her; one live prisoner. All Section chiefs report to me on the Bridge on the triple."

"Thomas," I said, "go down in the lift and open up for the Chiefs. Here's the release key for the combination; you know how to operate it?"

"Sure, Cap'n; but are you sure you want to let them boys in here after the way they jumped you an' all?"

I opened my mouth to answer, but he beat me to it. "Fergit I asked ya that, Cap'n, pleasir. You ain't been wrong yet."

"It's O.K., Thomas," I said. "There won't be any more trouble."

Epilogue

On the eve of the twentieth anniversary of Reunion Day, a throng of well-heeled celebrants filled the dining room and overflowed onto the terraces of the Star Tower Dining Room, from whose 5,700 foot height above the beaches, the Florida Keys, a hundred miles to the south, were visible on clear days.

The Era reporter stood beside the vast glass entry way surveying the crowd, searching for celebrities from whom he might elicit bits of color to spice the day's transmission.

At the far side of the room, surrounded by chattering admirers, stood the Ambassador from the New Terran Federation; a portly, graying, jolly ex-Naval officer. A minor actress passed at close range, looking the other way. A cabinet member stood at the bar talking earnestly to a ball player, ignoring a group of hopeful reporters and fans.

The Era stringer, an experienced hand, passed over the hard pressed VIP's near the center of the room and started a face-by-face check of the less gregarious diners seated at obscure tables along the sides of the room.

He was in luck; the straight-backed gray-haired figure in the dark civilian suit, sitting alone at a tiny table in an alcove, caught his eye. He moved closer, straining for a clear glimpse through the crowd. Then he was sure. He had the biggest possible catch of the day in his sights; Admiral of Fleets Frederick Greylorn.

The reporter hesitated; he was well aware of the Admiral's reputation for near-absolute silence on the subject of his already legendary cruise, the fabulous voyage of the Galahad. He couldn't just barge in on the Admiral and demand answers, as was usual with publicity-hungry politicians and show people. He could score the biggest story of the century today; but he had to hit him right.

You couldn't hope to snow a man like the Admiral; he wasn't somebody you could push around. You could sense the solid iron of him from here.

Nobody else had noticed the solitary diner. The Era man drifted closer, moving unhurriedly, thinking furiously. It was no good trying some tricky approach; his best bet was the straight-from-the-shoulder bit. No point in hesitating. He stopped beside the table.

The Admiral was looking out across the Gulf. He turned and glanced up at the reporter.

The news man looked him squarely in the eye. "I'm a reporter, Admiral," he said. "Will you talk to me?"

The Admiral nodded to the seat across from him. "Sit down," he said. He glanced around the room.

The reporter caught the look. "I'll keep it light, sir," he said. "I don't want company either." That was being frank.

"You want the answers to some questions, don't you?" the Admiral said.

"Why, yes, sir," the reporter said. He started to inconspicuously key his pocket recorder, but caught himself. "May I record your remarks, Admiral?" he said. Frankness all the way.

"Go ahead," said the Admiral.

"Now, Admiral," the reporter began, "the Terran public has of course ..."

"Never mind the patter, son," the Admiral said mildly. "I know what the questions are. I've read all the memoirs of the crew. They've been coming out at the rate of about two a year for some time now. I had my own reasons for not wanting to add anything to my official statement."

The Admiral poured wine into his glass. "Excuse me," he said. "Will you join me?" He signalled the waiter.

"Another wine glass, please," he said. He looked at the golden wine in the glass, held it up to the light. "You know, the Florida wines are as good as any in the world," he said. "That's not to say the California and Ohio wines aren't good. But this Flora Pinellas is a genuine original, not an imitation Rhine; and it compares favorably with the best of the old vintages, particularly the '87."

The glass arrived and the waiter poured. The reporter had the wit to remain silent.

"The first question is usually, how did I know I could take the Mancji ship. After all, it was big, vast. It loomed over us like a mountain. The Mancji themselves weighed almost two tons each; they liked six gee gravity. They blasted our communication off the air, just for practice. They talked big, too. We were invaders in their territory. They were amused by us. So where did I get the notion that our attack would be anything more than a joke to them? That's the big question." The Admiral shook his head.

"The answer is quite simple. In the first place, they were pulling six gees by using a primitive dumbbell configuration. The only reason for that type of layout, as students of early space vessel design can tell you, is to simplify setting up a gee field effect using centrifugal force. So they obviously had no gravity field generators.

"Then their transmission was crude. All they had was simple old-fashioned short-range radio, and even that was noisy and erratic. And their reception was as bad. We had to use a kilowatt before they could pick it up at 200 miles. We didn't know then it was all organically generated; that they had no equipment."

The Admiral sipped his wine, frowning at the recollection. "I was pretty sure they were bluffing when I changed course and started after them. I had to hold our acceleration down to two and a half gees because I had to be able to move around the ship. And at that acceleration we gained on them. They couldn't beat us. And it wasn't because they couldn't take high gees; they liked six for comfort, you remember. No, they just didn't have the power."

The Admiral looked out the window.

"Add to that the fact that they apparently couldn't generate ordinary electric current. I admit that none of this was conclusive, but after all, if I was wrong we were sunk anyway. When Thomas told me the nature of the damage to our radar and communications systems, that was another hint. Their big display of Mancji power was just a blast of radiation right across the communication spectrum; it burned tubes and blew fuses; nothing else. We were back in operation an hour after our attack.

"The evidence was there to see, but there's something about giant size that gets people rattled. Size alone doesn't mean a thing. It's rather like the bluff the Soviets ran on the rest of the world for a couple of decades back in the war era, just because they sprawled across half the globe. They were a giant, though it was mostly frozen desert. When the showdown came they didn't have it. They were a pushover.

"All right, the next question is why did I choose H. E. instead of going in with everything I had? That's easy, too. What I wanted was information, not revenge. I still had the heavy stuff in reserve and ready to go if I needed it, but first I had to try to take them alive. Vaporizing them wouldn't have helped our position. And I was lucky; it worked.

"The, ah, confusion below evaporated as soon as the Section chiefs got a look at the screens and realized that we had actually knocked out the Mancji. We matched speeds with the wreckage and the patrols went out to look for a piece of ship with a survivor in it. If we'd had no luck we would have tackled the other half of the ship, which was still intact and moving off fast. But we got quite a shock when we found the nature of the wreckage." The Admiral grinned.

"Of course today everybody knows all about the Mancji hive intelligence, and their evolutionary history. But we were pretty startled to find that the only wreckage consisted of the Mancji themselves, each two-ton slug in his own hard chitin shell. Of course, a lot of the cells were ruptured by the explosions, but most of them had simply disassociated from the hive mass as it broke up. So there was no ship; just a cluster of cells like a giant bee hive, and mixed up among the slugs, the damnedest collection of loot you can imagine. The odds and ends they'd stolen and tucked away in the hive during a couple hundred years of camp-following.

"The patrols brought a couple of cells alongside, and Mannion went out to try to establish contact. Sure enough, he got a very faint transmission, on the same bands as before. The cells were talking to each other in their own language. They ignored Mannion even though his transmission must have blanketed everything within several hundred miles. We eventually brought one of them into the cargo lock and started trying different wave-lengths on it. Then Kramer had the idea of planting a couple of electrodes and shooting a little juice to it. Of course, it loved the DC, but as soon as we tried AC, it gave up. So we had a long talk with it and found out everything we needed to know.

"It was a four-week run to the nearest outpost planet of the New Terran Federation, and they took me on to New Terra aboard one of their fast liaison vessels. The rest you know. We, the home planet, were as lost to the New Terrans as they were to us. They greeted us as though we were their own ancestors come back to visit them.

"Most of my crew, for personal reasons, were released from duty there, and settled down to stay.

"The clean-up job here on Earth was a minor operation to their Navy. As I recall, the trip back was made in a little over five months, and the Red Tide was killed within four weeks of the day the task force arrived. I don't think they wasted a motion. One explosive charge per cell, of just sufficient size to disrupt the nucleus. When the critical number of cells had been killed, the rest died overnight.

"It was quite a different Earth that emerged from under the plague, though. You know it had taken over all of the land area except North America and a strip of Western Europe, and all of the sea it wanted. It was particularly concentrated over what had been the jungle areas of South America, Africa, and Asia. You must realize that in the days before the Tide, those areas were almost completely uninhabitable. You have no idea what the term Jungle really implied. When the Tide died, it disintegrated into its component molecules; and the result was that all those vast fertile Jungle lands were now beautifully levelled and completely cleared areas covered with up to twenty feet of the richest topsoil imaginable. That was what made it possible for old Terra to become what she is today; the Federation's truck farm, and the sole source of those genuine original Terran foods that all the rest of the worlds pay such fabulous prices for.

"Strange how quickly we forget. Few people today remember how we loathed and feared the Tide when we were fighting it. Now it's dismissed as a blessing in disguise."

The Admiral paused. "Well," he said, "I think that answers the questions and gives you a bit of homespun philosophy to go with it."

"Admiral," said the reporter, "you've given the public some facts it's waited a long time to hear. Coming from you, sir, this is the greatest story that could have come out of this Reunion Day celebration. But there is one question more, if I may ask it. Can you tell me, Admiral, just how it was that you rejected what seemed to be prima facie proof of the story the Mancji told; that they were the lords of creation out there, and that humanity was nothing but a tame food animal to them?"

The Admiral sighed. "I guess it's a good question," he said. "But there was nothing supernatural about my figuring that one. I didn't suspect the full truth, of course. It never occurred to me that we were the victims of the now well-known but still inexplicable sense of humor of the Mancji, or that they were nothing but scavengers around the edges of the Federation. The original Omega ship had met them and seen right through them.

"Well, when this hive spotted us coming in, they knew enough about New Terra to realize at once that we were strangers, coming from outside the area. It appealed to their sense of humor to have the gall to strut right out in front of us and try to put over a swindle. What a laugh for the oyster kingdom if they could sell Terrans on the idea that they were the master race. It never occurred to them that we might be anything but Terrans; Terrans who didn't know the Mancji. And they were canny enough to use an old form of Interlingua; somewhere they'd met men before.

"Then we needed food. They knew what we ate, and that was where they went too far. They had, among the flotsam in their hive, a few human bodies they had picked up from some wreck they'd come across in their travels. They had them stashed away like everything else they could lay a pseudopod on. So they stacked them the way they'd seen Terran frozen foods shipped in the past, and sent them over. Another of their little jokes.

"I suppose if you're already overwrought and eager to quit, and you've been badly scared by the size of an alien ship, it's pretty understandable that the sight of human bodies, along with the story that they're just a convenient food supply, might seem pretty convincing. But I was already pretty dubious about the genuineness of our pals, and when I saw those bodies it was pretty plain that we were hot on the trail of Omega Colony. There was no other place humans could have come from out there. We had to find out the location from the Mancji."

"But, Admiral," said the reporter, "true enough they were humans, and presumably had some connection with the colony, but they were naked corpses stacked like cordwood. The Mancji had stated that these were slaves, or rather domesticated animals; they wouldn't have done you any good."

"Well, you see, I didn't believe that," the Admiral said. "Because it was an obvious lie. I tried to show some of the officers, but I'm afraid they weren't being too rational just then.

"I went into the locker and examined those bodies; if Kramer had looked closely, he would have seen what I did. These were no tame animals. They were civilized men."

"How could you be sure, Admiral? They had no clothing, no identifying marks, nothing. Why didn't you believe they were cattle?"

"Because," said the Admiral, "all the men had nice neat haircuts."

www.ingramcontent.com/pod-product-compliance
Lightning Source LLC
Chambersburg PA
CBHW020640130626
46552CB00003B/1319